Abella Starts a Tooth Fairy School

By Zane Carson Carruth

Abella Starts a Tooth Fairy School

Printed in the United States of America
Originally published, 2020
ISBN #: 978-0-692-13281-4
Library of Congress Control Number #2020911573
Published by Carson Marketing, LLC
5110 San Felipe St., Houston, Texas 77056
www.carsonmarketing.com
www.worldsfirsttoothfairy.com
Illustrations by BTween Animations
Prepared for publication by Sheri Siebert, Jostens
Printed by Jostens Printing & Publishing, USA

Publisher's Cataloging-In-Publication Data
(Prepared by The Donohue Group, Inc.)

Names: Carruth, Zane Carson, author. | BTween Animations (Firm), illustrator.
Title: Abella starts a tooth fairy school / by Zane Carson Carruth ; [illustrations by BTween Animations].
Description: Houston, Texas : Carson Marketing, LLC, [2020] | Series: [The world's first tooth fairy ... ever] ; [3] | Interest age level: 003-008. | Summary: "Word has spread far and wide through Tulip Hollow about the shiny tooth Abella brought back from her recent adventure ... Overwhelmed by the demand, Abella realizes she must start a professional tooth fairy school to train all the other fairies to be a tooth fairy"-- Provided by publisher.
Identifiers: ISBN 9780692132814
Subjects: LCSH: Fairies--Training of--Juvenile fiction. | Schools--Juvenile fiction. | Courage--Juvenile fiction. | CYAC: Fairies--Fiction. | Schools--Fiction. | Courage--Fiction.
Classification: LCC PZ7.1.C4268 Ab 2020 | DDC [E]--dc23

This book is dedicated with love to my daughter, Brittany,
grandchildren Chloe, Carson and Truett.
And always and forever, in loving memory of my son, Chad.

*L*ocated deep in the forest was a secret world called Tulip Hollow. It was the home of a young fairy named Abella. She lived in a castle with her mom, dad, and brother Gage. Abella was known everywhere as the fairy that began the tooth fairy tradition.

After Abella's big adventure in the forest and bringing home a pearly white tooth, everyone was frantic to have one. "Please, Abella, will you get me one?" asked a friend. "Me too!" said another.

Overwhelmed by her friends' excitement, Abella thought, I need to open a tooth fairy school! And this is just what she did.

The first day of class was buzzing with excitement. Her best friend, Darcie, her brother Gage, and the Clark brothers were there, among others.

As Abella organized the classroom, the students were getting antsy. The Clark brothers and Gage chased each other around the room making everyone laugh.

"OK, let's get started!" she exclaimed. "What does a tooth fairy need to be successful?" she asked.

"A baseball!" the Clark brothers shouted.

"Rollerblades!" Gage bellowed and everyone giggled.

Abella rolled her eyes and sighed. "No, you need to know where to find the tooth."

Abella explained that every tooth brought back to Tulip Hollow becomes magical after it is sprinkled with fairy dust. Then she pulled a tooth out of her pocket and said, "Look, watch this."

She threw a handful of fairy dust in the air. As the dust landed on the tooth, it lit up, vibrated, and turned beautiful colors.

"Show me a tooth under a pillow," she told the tooth. Magically, a vision appeared of a little girl slipping her tooth under her pillow.

Everyone gasped and stared in awe.
Abella said, "The tooth will guide you to the pillow. However, you must be careful and guard it with your life. Once the fairy dust lands on the tooth, it becomes extremely powerful."

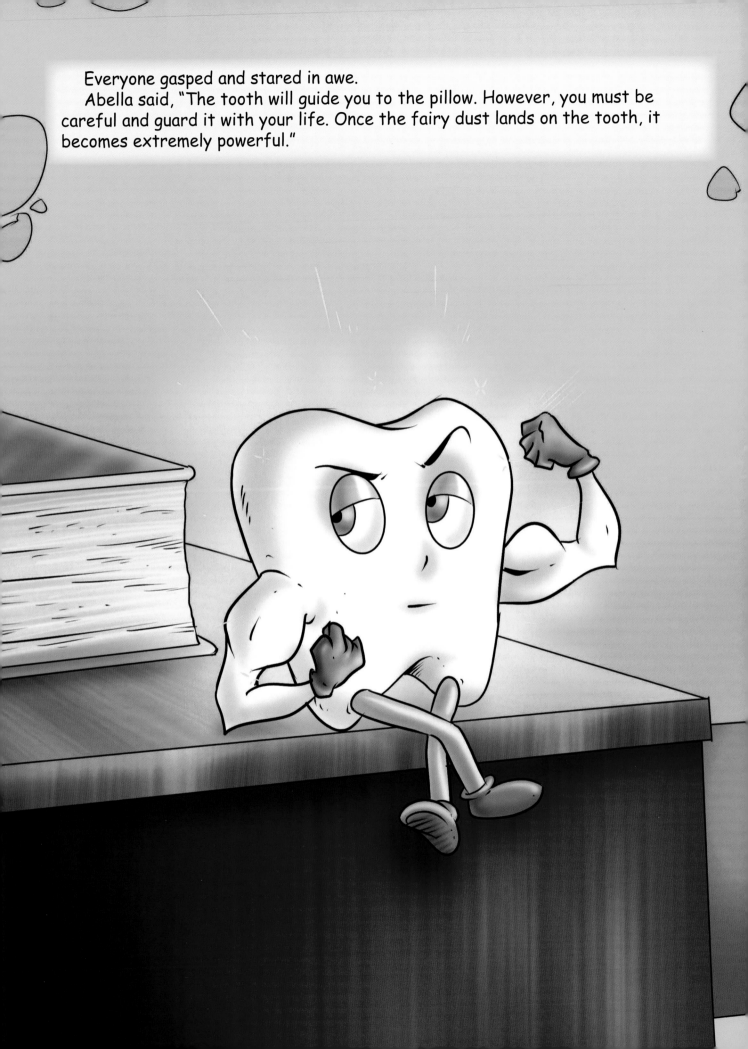

"Next, you will need a dollar bill," Abella said.

"Why do we need it?" asked Darcie.

"Because we leave a dollar bill under the pillow in exchange for the tooth," explained Abella.

"Where do we get a dollar bill?" asked Gage.

All the fairies jumped up and ran outside. "Look," said Darcie. She pointed to a dollar bill on the tree.

One of the Clark brothers leaned down and tugged at a leaf. "Ouch, I'm a flower. I'm not made of money!" exclaimed the little flower.
"Sorry," mumbled the Clark boy.

By the end of class, the students were ready to begin their journey as professional tooth fairies. Abella handed each fairy a magic tooth. And they were off!

"Come on, Darcie, let's get this adventure started!" Abella exclaimed. They soon zeroed in on a little boy who had slipped his tooth under his pillow.

Abella pointed to him and whispered to Darcie, "You go first." Darcie smiled and gently flitted downward. After she slid the tooth from under the pillow, she replaced it with a dollar bill.

Abella grinned and gave Darcie a thumbs up. The fairies nodded to each other and flew out the window giggling.

Then, it was Abella's turn. Although Abella was a certified professional tooth fairy, she was not prepared for what happened next.

Very quietly, Abella fluttered to the pillow and was about to slide her hand under it when she heard a low growl: "Grrrrr, grrrrr!" Abella stopped, her heart pounding as she slowly turned her head to the side. Yikes, there was a dog by the bed!

Abella shot Darcie a horrified look and pointed to the open window. "Goooooooo, Darcie!" she yelled. They flew out the window as fast as they could, as the dog chased after them.

Flying as far from the house as possible, they stopped to rest on a tree branch. Abella and Darcie looked at each other in shock and disbelief. "That was close!" they both exclaimed at the same time.

Unfortunately, they did not see the squirrel named Pearl sneak up on them. Abella felt the limb move and froze when she saw Pearl. She had heard about Pearl and immediately felt threatened. Abella tried to sound courageous when she said sternly, "Get out of here! Beat it! Scram!"

Pearl snickered and replied, "Not so fast, little fairy. I know you have a magic tooth in your bag, and I want it. I need it to tell me where the other squirrels have hidden their nuts for the winter. You see, I've not had a very good year collecting food for the winter. I've been really busy being really busy. It isn't easy being me," she sighed.

Abella clutched her bag tightly and gave Pearl a cold look. She said forcefully, "No Pearl, I worked hard for this magic tooth. I am not giving it to you so you can steal other squirrels' food."

Pearl lunged at Abella, knocking the magic tooth out of her bag. It fell to the ground and quick as lightning, Pearl was on the ground, ready to grab it.

Swoosh! Suddenly, a big red bird swooped down, picked up the tooth, and chased Pearl away. The red bird had been perched in the tree and heard everything.

He flew to Abella and dropped the tooth in her lap. "Thank you, Mr. Red Bird!" Abella exclaimed. He turned and winked at her as he flew away.

Happy to have completed their first day as tooth fairies, Abella and Darcie were ready to fly home.

WELCOME TO TULIP HOLLOW
HOME OF THE
WORLD'S FIRST TOOTH FAIRY

Abella smiled as she looked down and saw the moonlight illuminating a big sign her students had built in her honor.

About the Author, *Zane Carson Carruth*

Zane and her husband Brady reside in Houston, Texas. She is actively involved in the Houston Grand Opera, Houston SPCA and the Discovery Green Conservancy. In addition to owning Carson Marketing, LLC, Ms. Carruth is a certified etiquette and protocol professional and has published articles in several high-profile magazines. Her first book titled *The World's First Tooth Fairy...Ever*, published in 2016, is a trademarked series about the tooth fairy. *The World's First Tooth Fairy... Ever* and *The Adventures of Abella and Her Magic Wand* have both won the Story Monsters Seal of Approval. When not traveling, she cherishes spending time with her 3 grandchildren, Chloe, Carson and Truett.

www.carsonmarketing.com
www.etiquettetoexcel.com
www.worldsfirsttoothfairy.com